TEAMWORK!

BRAVERY!

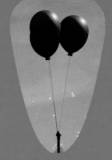

PATIENCE!

PATIENCE!

SHARING!

GIVING!

PJMASKS

We're on Our Way!

PaRragon

Bath • New York • Cologne • Melbourne • Delhi
Hong Kong • Shenzhen • Singapore

TEAMWORK!

The sports equipment has gone missing! At night, the PJ Masks set out to find the culprit so they can save Sports Day.

Night Ninja and his Ninjalinos have taken all the sports gear. Gekko tries to get everything back by himself, but he discovers that he's stronger when he works as part of a team with Catboy and Owlette. Together, they manage to save the day!

BRAVERY!

During practice for the school dance, everyone laughs when Connor falls trying the Spinning Tornado move. He's too afraid to keep trying. Luna Girl's moths arrive. . . .

Find the stickers that complete each scene.

Luna Girl drops a giant dome to trap the PJ Masks! To free them, Catboy has to get brave and perform the Spinning Tornado move to dig a hole out under the dome!

PATIENCE!

The Fairground Flyer, the new train at the fair, has disappeared! That night, the PJ Masks set out to find it.

Find the stickers that complete each scene.

Romeo has stolen the train, and an impatient Owlette springs into action by herself. She needs to be patient enough to work with Catboy and Gekko. Together, they stop Romeo and return the train to the fair.

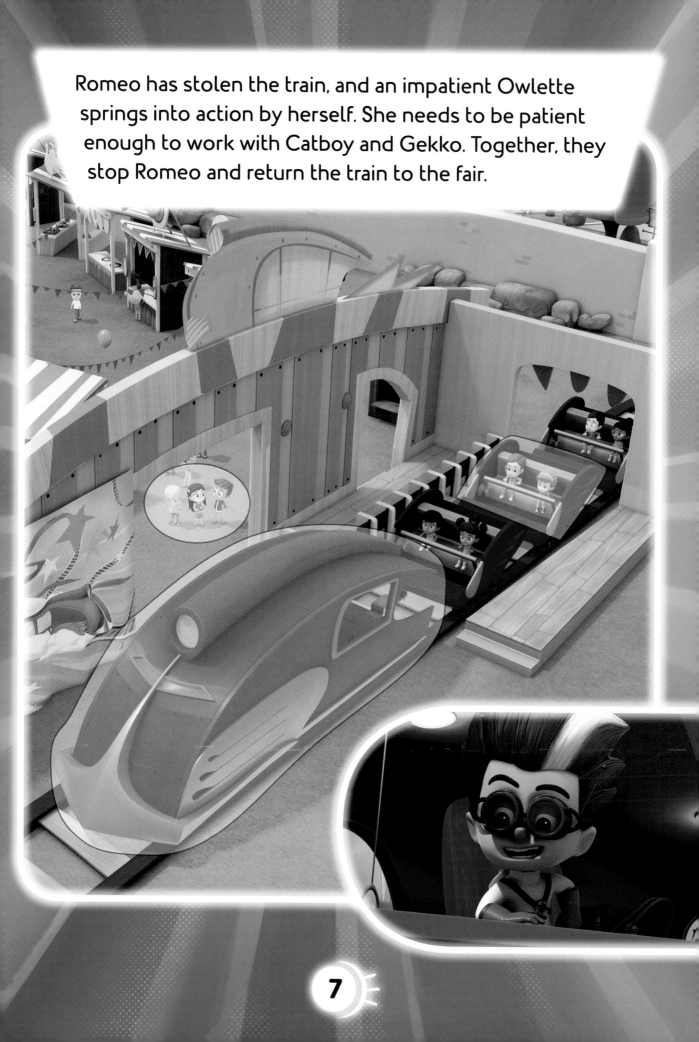

SHARING!

Romeo uses a giant pair of boxing gloves attached to his lab to break into the museum. When one breaks off, Catboy uses it to try to bounce after him, but he can't control it on his own. . . .

After Gekko's jet pack fails, Catboy shares the pogo dozer with him. Together, they are able to control it to stop Romeo!

GIVING!

Amaya decides to bring her beloved Giving
Owl statue to show-and-tell. Luna Girl likes
the statue, too. So much so that she takes it!

Luna Girl loves the Giving Owl more than all the other things put together. But Owlette wants her statue back.

Owlette learns it's better to give than receive and she lets Luna Girl keep the Giving Owl statue. So, Luna Girl gives back the class's things for their show-and-tell!

Find the stickers that complete each scene.

Connor is getting ready to turn into Catboy! Find and circle the two images of Connor that are exactly the same.

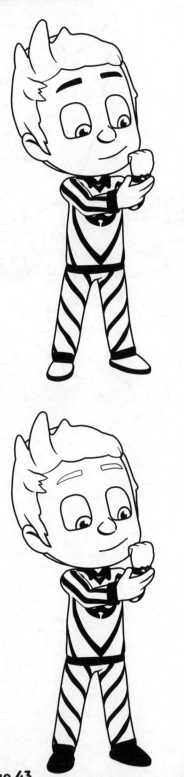

Answer on page 43

Draw a line between Amaya, Connor, and Greg and the heroes they become!

Answers on page 43

Draw Catboy's badge.
Use the picture as a guide.

Get Gekko to his Gekko-Mobile as quickly as you can!

START

FINISH

Answer on page 43

17

Connect the dots so Owlette can fly off into the night to save the day!

2

B

1

A

3

C

D

4

E

5

G

F

7

6

I

9

H

8

Answer on page 43

Gekko is super strong! Draw some heavy things for him to lift!

Catboy can hear things from very far away!
Fill in the blanks of some things his cat
ears can detect that others can't hear.
Use the word bar for clues.

| purr | growl | chirp | oink |

1. Catboy can hear a pig _____ from far away.

2. Catboy can hear a cat _____ from miles away.

3. Catboy can pick up a bird's _____ when no one else can.

4. A dog's _____ will never go undetected by Catboy!

Answers on page 43

Owlette has super eyesight! She can see
very small things from very far away.
Draw some small things you think
she might see when she's flying!

Unscramble the words below to find out what Romeo longs to do.

leru   het   drowl

- - - -   - - -   - - - - - -

Answer on page 43

What time is it?
It's time to be a hero!

Oh no! Night Ninja has thrown Sticky-Splats everywhere! Fill this page with Sticky-Splats and then color them in.

Luna Girl uses her Luna-Magnet to get things to come her way!

The PJ Masks have sent Romeo running away in defeat. Find the path to get him back to his lab.

FINISH

A
B
C

START

Answer on page 43

If you joined the PJ Masks, what would your mask look like? Draw and color it!

Draw a line between each villain and their helper.

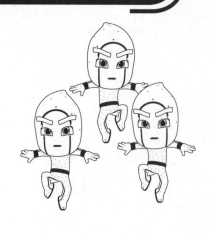

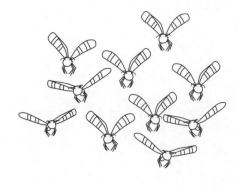

Answers on page 43

Draw and color what your badge would look like if you became a new member of the PJ Masks!

Connect the dots to see where the PJ Masks go at the start of each mission.

8

11

9

10

7

12

13

6

3 2

17 16

5

4

15

14

1

18

Answer on page 43

Night Ninja and his Ninjalinos have stolen Gekko's birthday cake! Can you find four differences between the two pictures?

Answers on page 44

Draw your favorite PJ Masks character defeating one of the villains.

Help the PJ Masks find the villains and their helpers hidden in the puzzle below.
Look up, down, backward, and diagonally.

O L R I G A N U L H
Y E B A X J I D H X
W Y M E W N N Q T X
R I H O S I J Y O W
W N Z H R N A Z B H
D O T A F T L T O D
M O Q L H H I J R B
M E J N O G N Z H C
H S N H E I O X Q J
X V Q B B N S C Y V

Romeo   Moths
Robot   Night Ninja
Luna Girl   Ninjalinos

33

Answers on page 44

Gekko is determined to stop Romeo from icing over the whole city! Help him by matching up the pieces to complete the picture.

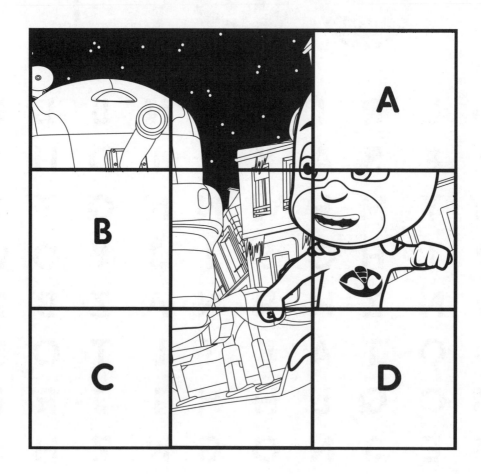

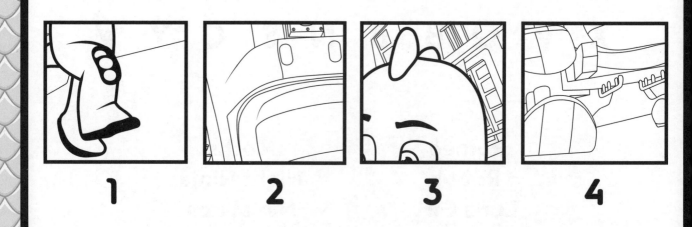

1   2   3   4

Answers on page 44

Color in the spaces with the dots.
Who do you see?

Answers on page 44

Owlette has to stop Luna Girl's evil Moonflower from spreading its seeds and turning the city into weeds! Find the right path to get Owlette to the fiendish flower.

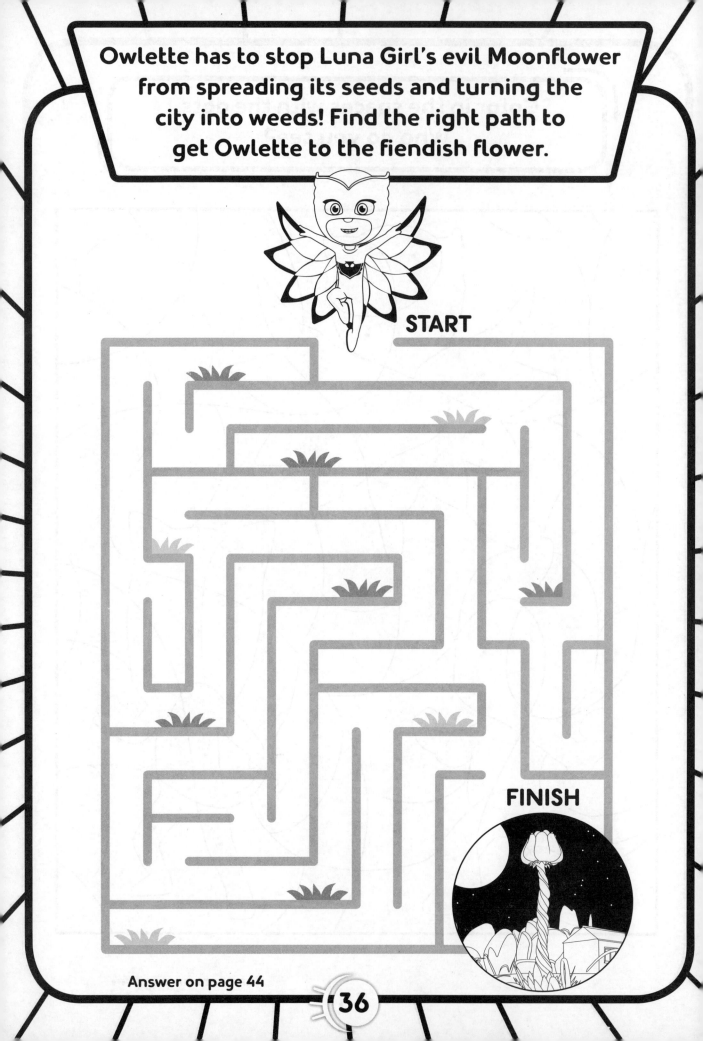

START

FINISH

Answer on page 44

Find the right word in the clue bar to complete each sentence.

eyes	leaps	rush

1. Gekko is always ready to _____ into danger.

2. Keep your _____ on Owlette!

3. Catboy _____ to the rescue!

Answers on page 44

Can you spot three differences between the two pictures?

Answers on page 44

Use this code to find out how Owlette sends villains flying.

1	2	3	4	5	6	7
d	g	i	l	n	o	w

6 7 4　　7 3 5 2　　7 3 5 1

Answer on page 44

Catboy stops Night Ninja from ruining the parade! Draw a line from the close-ups below to where they appear in the picture.

When the sun comes up, Connor, Amaya, and Greg are ready for another day!

ANSWERS

Page 14

Page 15

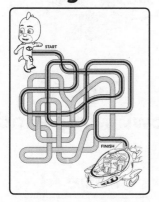

Page 17

Page 18

Page 20
1. oink
2. purr
3. chirp
4. growl

Page 22
rule the world

Page 26
Path C

Page 28

Page 30

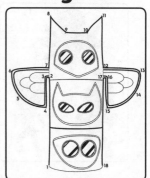

ANSWERS

Page 31

Page 33

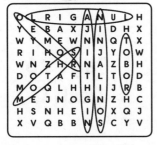

Page 34

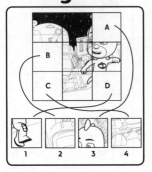

Page 35

Page 36

Page 37

1. rush   2. eyes   3. leaps

Page 38

Page 40

owl wing wind

Page 41

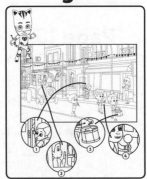